# The **Varmint** and Other **Short Stories**

FAYE RAPOPORT DESPRES

Published by Huntsville Independent Press

*103 Spenryn Drive, Madison, AL 35758*

The Varmint and Other Short Stories is a work of creative nonfiction based on the author's personal experiences and perspectives. Names and details may have been altered for privacy. The opinions expressed are those of the author and do not necessarily reflect the views of the publisher.



Huntsville Independent Press can bring authors to your live event. For more information or to book an event, contact Huntsville Independent Press at +1 (256) 678-0411 or visit our website at www.HuntsvilleIndependent.com.

Cover design by Olayemi Bolaji
Interior design by 3 Dog Creative

The text for this book was set in Dutch Mediaeval Pro.

Manufactured in the United States of America
First HIP paperback edition December 2024

12345678910

The Library of Congress has cataloged the hardcover edition as follows:

**Names:** DesPres, Faye Rapoport, author.

**Title:** The Varmint and Other Short Stories

LCCN (2024950415)
Identifiers: ISBN 9798990504936 (pbk)

# PREVIOUSLY PUBLISHED

Thank you to the editors who first published these works.

"The Varmint" first appeared in Connotation Press: An Online Artifact.

"Capture the Moon" first appeared in Red Earth Review

"Who Let the Cats Out" first appeared in Mystery Times Ten 2013, published by Buddhapuss Ink, and was anthologized in Nine Daily Lives, published by Prarie Rose Publications/Five Star Press.

# Contents

# Foreword from the Author

Fiction. Some readers are surprised that I write it, because my first book, *Message from a Blue Jay*, is a collection of personal essays. In fact, when I earned my MFA in Creative Writing, I focused on creative nonfiction.

So, where did these three fictions come from?

I've always been a multi-genre writer. As a teenager, I wrote stories about twins named Karen and Karena. The stories had a reader of one: a childhood friend. I also wrote poetry that's embarrassing to read now, although my poetry skills improved after years of practice and study, including poetry writing courses I took at The New School and the State University of New York at Albany. In fact, my first literary publications were poems. It was only after working as a journalist that I fell into—and focused on—creative nonfiction.

Then one day, after I'd been writing personal essays for a good six or seven years, something just hit me. An idea came totally from my imagination. I started writing.

"Who Let the Cats Out?" flowed from my mind through my fingers onto the page with almost no effort. The story won third place out of 200 entries in a mystery writing contest and was anthologized in two published books. Then another idea came. Then another. Each story came knocking on my door (or my head), asking to be told.

Before I knew it, I had written and published three short stories, different in theme and tone, each poured onto the page from an idea. Usually something in "real life" inspired that idea—most often a person (or cat) who prompted the basic concept for a character. After that, everything was fiction. This was so different from my process for writing creative nonfiction. My personal essays require careful consideration of true-life events, numerous drafts, and often many months of revision and editing before they feel "right."

Fiction, for me, feels more like play. Fiction feels fun.

Each of the three stories you'll find in these pages was published by a literary journal, but the stories have never been available as a collection (albeit a small one) for a larger readership until now. I want to thank Joshua Adams, Senior Editor of Huntsville Independent Press, for making that happen.

I hope these stories touch your heart and entertain you... until the next tale comes knocking, asking to be told.

*- Faye Rapoport DesPres*

# THE VARMINT

Paddy tended to his garden in the late afternoons, when the hot sun stopped blazing through the maple tree that stood smack in the middle of the back fence, or the cherry tree trapped in the corner of the yard, or the phone wires blocking the view of the sky. If he ventured out before 4 o'clock, his shirt got soaked through before he could pull all the weeds or unwind the long hose from the plastic reel Janie had installed. Paddy had harrumphed as his eldest daughter hooked one end of the reel to the outside faucet and the other to the hose. She insisted that the hose was a hazard. After eighty-one years, fifty of them living in this small house with Alice, Paddy figured he knew how to avoid tripping over a hose. Janie was adamant, though. She was as stubborn as the varmint that lived under the toolshed, and Paddy had learned to pick his battles. So he sat in his tattered, old fold-out chair and watched as Janie wound the hose onto the reel. She coiled it slowly, all neat and tidy. Behind her, the varmint poked its head out of its hole. *I may not be standing up to Janie*, Paddy thought, *but you can be sure I'll get the better of that varmint.*

Paddy planted the same assortment of vegetables every year: cucumbers, squash, peas, some lettuce, eggplants, and too many tomatoes. There was a time when he grew pumpkins, but he'd given up on that. Back then, the kids watched as Paddy rolled the biggest pumpkins away from the vines so each child could choose a favorite to carve for Halloween. Now, his and Alice's kids all had children of their own, and they bought their Halloween pumpkins at the supermarket.

Tomatoes were another story. Paddy was well-known for the quality of his tomatoes.

They always ripened to a round, bright red. Toward the end of every summer, Alice divided the extras into used plastic grocery bags and hung them on their neighbors' front doorknobs. Of course, a few things had changed since Paddy and Alice moved onto the street. Four of the newer houses hadn't been built when they bought theirs, and over time some of the neighbors had moved away. Two of the oldest residents had died. These days, new people moving into the neighborhood didn't stop by to say hello or introduce themselves. Alice still hung tomatoes on a few of the front doorknobs, but she also made tomato sauce to store in the freezer and gave extra bags of tomatoes to the kids.

The varmint showed up early that spring. Paddy spotted it chewing on his pea plants one morning and rushed outside yelling, with his hands in the air. The varmint, which was actually a large, brown groundhog, glanced up and continued its chewing. But when the old man barreled closer, the animal bolted from the peas and squeezed its rotund body under the short wire fence Paddy had built years ago to keep the rabbits out. The varmint sprinted toward the toolshed with the old man on its tail and dove into a large, round hole. Paddy leaned over and examined the hole. The dirt around it was freshly dug, meaning the varmint had just moved in.

Cursing, Paddy stomped back to the house to tell Alice.

"Oh, no you won't," Alice said, as she placed a bowl of soup and a glass filled with water on the kitchen table.

Paddy sat heavily in his chair. Alice was seventy-six, five years younger than Paddy, and it was she who had insisted he go to the doctor last December. His hand had been trembling for six months by then, and he had started to have some trouble walking. His walk had become more of a shuffle. He and Alice hadn't talked much about the diagnosis.

"It's the only way," Paddy said.

"No one is poisoning anything," Alice said.

"That darn thing will eat all my vegetables," Paddy insisted.

"Or every neighbor's cat and every squirrel will get poisoned," Alice said.

Husbands listen more than you'd think. Paddy didn't answer; he just stared at the chicken noodle soup in the bowl on the table. Then he picked up his spoon and tried to manage the trembling as he filled the spoon and lifted it toward his mouth. Alice stood and watched him, her hands resting behind her on the Formica countertop next to the sink. She wore an off-white sweatshirt patterned with tangled blue flowers and blue cotton pants. Her hair was short and white, and it curled around plastic-framed glasses. Alice had always been taller than Paddy, but lately it seemed that either she was getting taller or he was getting smaller.

"Damn spoon," Paddy said, as he spilled soup onto the table.

"We'll see what the doctor says Tuesday," Alice said, pronouncing it *Tues*-dee. "Janie said she'd drive us over to the VA."

Paddy fixed his piercing blue eyes on the spoon. He said, with a voice turned gravelly with age, "A lot of good the doctor'll do." Then he maneuvered another spoonful of soup toward his mouth.

Alice glanced out the window and spotted the groundhog. It was standing near the shed, munching on fresh grass. She looked back at Paddy, but he hadn't seen the creature so she walked over to the window and pulled the curtains closed.

"That sun," Alice said. "It gets so hot now."

Paddy and Alice were born and raised in this town before anyone started calling it a city. They remembered when the streets were surrounded by farmland, and the redbrick mills in the center of town buzzed with workers. Back then, the rectangular buildings down by the river housed a factory for a World War II defense contractor. Paddy and Alice had raised four children, two boys and two girls. They remembered when the laughter of their children filled the summers, and when fall meant raking leaves and jumping into the piles. Back then, the snow fell from December through March. Paddy bought two wooden sleds with steel runners so the kids could slide from the top of the hill to the bottom, straight through all the backyards. Sometimes they were joined by two brothers who lived in the house just down the hill. Those boys were long gone now; one joined the army right out of high school, and the other landed in trouble because of drugs. A few years ago, the parents sold the house to a lady who bought it as an investment and rented it to a couple that had two BMWs.

Changes can snowball faster than you'd think. On the other side of Paddy and Alice's house, a developer split a property into two housing plots and built a crappy modular home next to Paddy and Alice. Sometimes Paddy felt like he'd gone to sleep one night and woken up the next day living in a place he didn't know.

Worst of all were the ugly fences. A town that once had farmland and rambling hills was now divided into squares of commercial and personal property protected by God-awful fences. They cropped up first around warehouses and parking lots and then separated the houses getting crowded by more houses. On the south side of town, where Paddy and Alice lived, most homeowners went cheap and put up chain link fences that turned orange with rust, making the streets look like they were lined with miniature prisons. At least on some of the side streets, people used real wood. Then came the white vinyl. The fences multiplied like rabbits, got taller every year, and now the backyards were guarded by six-foot walls.

Paddy hated the fences, but after a tide of developers rolled through the neighborhood and left more houses behind, he decided it was time to protect his and Alice's property. He and his eldest son, Peter, built a slatted wooden fence. Alice explained it to her quilting club this way: if Paddy couldn't control what was happening in the neighborhood, at least he could lord over their own little slice of heaven.

To Paddy and Alice, that's what their little house was. Paddy served as a gunner in World War II, and Alice spent those years working in a factory across the river that made parts for the Department of Defense. After the war ended and Paddy finally came home, he and Alice got married. He took a job with Public Works while Alice stayed home to raise the kids. Paddy held that job for forty-three years, retiring with a pension and a small golden clock, which they placed on their mantle.

Paddy wondered about the guys who ran the DPW now. He'd called five times since December about a pothole in front of the house that had knocked their Ford sedan out of alignment. The lady in the office kept promising to send a crew that never showed.

Paddy couldn't do anything about the pothole, he reasoned, but he damned well could do something about that varmint. He rarely admitted taking Alice's advice, but this time he called their younger son Michael, who lived up in New Hampshire with his wife and two kids, and asked him to drive down in his pick-up the next weekend to help build a better fence around the garden.

Fences are harder to build than you'd think. Michael rolled into the driveway the following Saturday morning and waited while his father pulled himself into the passenger seat.

They drove over to the hardware store on Main Street because Paddy said "those warehouse stores sell nothing but garbage."

Paddy trusted Bill, the owner of Mason's, although Bill had retired and the store was now run by Bill's son Kevin. Kevin showed Paddy and Michael some three-foot high, small-gauge rabbit fencing. They nodded their heads, and Michael loaded a thick roll onto the flatbed of his pickup, along with enough stakes to secure the fence every six feet.

Before getting started on their outdoor project, Michael stopped into the house to greet his mother. Alice was sitting on the couch in the living room sorting quilting squares on the coffee table with the television on. A local news anchor prattled on in the background, something about coyotes being sighted in the suburbs.

"Hi Mom," Michael said, leaning down and kissing Alice on the cheek.

Alice smiled up at her son and asked after his family. "Thank you for driving all the way down here," she said. "Look after your father. He's on one of his tirades."

Michael grinned and winked before heading back outside.

The job took five hours. Paddy kept two iron shovels in the shed, although their handles were splintered and the old blades were covered in rust. Michael put on cowhide leather work gloves and heaved one of the shovels in and out of the dirt, digging a foot-deep trench around the perimeter of the garden. Paddy stood nearby, leaning on the other shovel and pointing out spots his son had missed or not dug deep enough. When the sun got too hot, Michael shed his button-down work shirt and rubbed sunscreen on his torso. Alice brought out two filled water bottles.

"For heaven's sake, Dad, sit down," Alice said. She called Paddy "Dad" when the kids were around.

"A lot of good I'll do sitting in a chair," Paddy muttered.

"A lot of good you're doing standing around," Alice countered before heading back into the house.

That night Janie joined them for dinner, and then Michael headed upstairs to the bedroom he used to share with Peter. The next morning he drove back to New Hampshire, leaving his parents with a shiny new garden fence.

Groundhogs dig deeper than you'd think. That's what Ray, who lived across the street in the house with yellow siding and red wooden shutters, explained to Paddy a week later. Paddy discovered a tunnel under the new garden fence. "Adding insult to injury," as he put it when he told Ray, the varmint had destroyed half the remaining pea plants.

Ray ran his own tree cutting business and was twenty years younger than Paddy. His parents had raised him two houses down from the one he owned now. After Ray got married, he moved into his parents' basement. After he and his wife had a son and a daughter, he bought the yellow house at the top of the hill from an old man who wanted to get out from under his mortgage. When Ray's wife left, his grown kids lived in the house on and off. Mostly, Ray shared it with a boxer named Pinup. The name had a drinking story behind it.

Now Ray leaned against the cab of his truck, which had a "Raymond Boucher Tree Cutting" decal on the door, and chatted with Paddy about the groundhog.

"Damn varmint dug under the fence," Paddy said.

"They'll do that," Ray explained. "My aunt had one in her garden once, and every time we plugged up one of its holes, it just dug one somewhere else. Makes sense, if you think about it."

"Michael planted that fence a good foot in the ground. You'd think that would have stopped him," Paddy said.

"You'd think," Ray agreed, nodding amiably. "With my aunt, we tried that trick where you bend the fence at the bottom, so if they try to go under it, they hit the fence first. But—" Ray was a talker; Paddy knew if you let him go on, he'd talk for half an hour. So he cut Ray off. "Do you have some cement in your garage?" Paddy asked.

Ray had a garage full of tools and materials, and he was always willing to help a neighbor out.

"What for?" he asked Paddy.

"I figured I'd fill the tunnel with rocks and pour cement into it."

Ray cocked his head sideways, as if he wasn't sure Paddy heard the words out of his own mouth. "Well, you know that won't work," he said slowly. Then, speeding up, he began to explain. "He'll just dig a hole right next to it. We had a groundhog once at number 18," he pointed down the hill at the house he'd grown up in, "and my dad threatened to shoot it. My mom, well, you know," he threw his head back and laughed, "she loved animals, so *that* wasn't happening."

Ray looked around as if the comment had prompted a thought, stuck his fingers in his mouth, and whistled. Pinup came running from the other side of the house and leaped up, planting her legs on Ray's stomach.

Ray patted her head before gently pushing her off. "Stay where I can see you, Pinup," he said. Then he looked back at Paddy. "I remember my mom banging a spatula on the kitchen table and saying, 'Alexander Boucher, no way are you shooting that groundhog!' She thought the thing was cute. She wanted it to have cubs, or pups, or whatever you call them. That was before they built the house next door and we had—"

"Forget the cement," Paddy said. "Thanks anyway," and he turned to shuffle back across the street.

"You might want to try that thing about bending the bottom of the fence," Ray called after him. "Or Mason's sells Have-A-Hart traps."

Paddy paused halfway across the street, thought better of asking more, and shuffled on. Alice sat on the love seat in the small living room, examining a chosen quilting square. The television was on again.

"What did Ray say?" she asked without looking up.

"Cementing the hole won't work," Paddy said. "I knew it, of course."

"Of course," Alice said, staring harder at the strawberry-patterned fabric.

Live-trapping a groundhog is harder than you'd think. Two days later, Paddy stood at the kitchen table and examined his new Have-A-Hart trap. He'd found it at Mason's near a sign on another shelf that said "50% Off Snake Repellents."

Paddy spread the instructions out on the kitchen table. He read every word and examined the illustrations carefully. Paddy liked to know how things worked. He ran his trembling right hand over each of the trap's parts, slid the door up and down, and then tested the whole thing by setting the trigger platform and pressing on it gently. The door dropped onto his forearm.

*This should do it*, Paddy thought.

Back at Mason's, Kevin asked Paddy what he'd do after he caught the groundhog. Paddy explained that there was a big cemetery at the top of the hill, and he would release the varmint way on the other side.

"You're not allowed to do that," Kevin said.

"Why not?" Paddy demanded.

"There are laws," Kevin explained. "You can't trap wildlife and release it off your property."

Paddy stared hard at Kevin. "What about those companies that come to your house and trap the squirrels in your attic?" he asked. "That's what they do."

"No, they kill 'em," Kevin said. He placed his hands on the counter next to the cash register. "Euthanize 'em. Squirrels, raccoons, whatever they catch."

Paddy stared at Kevin for another moment. Then, without another word, he handed over the money and carried the trap out of the store.

Ray told Paddy that cantaloupe worked well for catching groundhogs. So Alice set out to buy a ripe cantaloupe at the super-sized supermarket across the river. The store had been built ten years before, and its paved parking lot went right up to the riverbank. The city constructed a fancy new footbridge right next to an old iron train bridge that no one ever bothered to take down.

The footbridge was two blocks from the bottom of the hill at the end of Paddy and Alice's street. The city council named it the Mary Benedict Bridge after the bossy old woman who lived with her daughter on the next street over, behind Paddy and Alice's house. Mary hounded the council about a new bridge for years, and when it finally got built she never tired of taking the credit. Not two weeks after the bridge naming ceremony, some kids painted graffiti all over the brass plaque. Paddy laughed when he heard this; he had been feuding with Mary since the time she took over the local paper route. She'd thrown Paddy's paper so far from his door—a little further every time he complained— that he'd ended up canceling his subscription. These days, Alice bought the paper at the supermarket.

When Paddy and Alice used to walk over the footbridge together, they'd stop in the middle and look out over the river. The water flowed east toward the big city harbor six miles away. Here, the riverbank was tangled with underbrush that grew beneath tall, old maples, oak trees, and pines. In the height of the summer, the trees in full leaf obscured the parking lots and warehouses. For those few blissful weeks, Paddy and Alice could stand in the center of the bridge and watch the water rush over an old, submerged dam where seagulls still perched, hoping to spot fish in the river. It was like nothing had changed in fifty years.

When Paddy was young, he fished in that river. Back then, Alice and her friends found places along the riverbank where the trees were especially thick. They made sure no one was around, and then stripped to their swimsuits and waded into the river under the hot summer sun. Now the water that curled over the old dam had a yellow-brown tinge, and formed a suspicious foam when it hit the rocks.

Three old tires and a supermarket cart lay half-buried in mud on the river bottom beneath the bridge. Sometimes an ancient snapping turtle moved slowly among the tires, as if looking for the river that used to be.

These days, Alice walked to the supermarket on her own. When she returned with a big, round cantaloupe, she endured Paddy's supervision as she cut the inside of the fruit into small, even cubes and set a pile on a paper towel for Paddy to carry out to the trap.

"It's silly to let good cantaloupe go to waste," Alice remarked as she slid the rest of the cantaloupe off the cutting board and into a large, white plastic mixing bowl. She'd combine it with strawberries and a banana to make fruit salad.

Paddy carried the cantaloupe cubes out to the trap, which he had placed in the middle of the remaining pea plants. Alice watched through the window as he checked to make sure the trigger was set, made his way out of the garden, and secured the make-shift gate. He stood for a while with his hands on his hips and surveyed his work. Then he looked over at the groundhog's hole beneath the shed and said something that Alice couldn't hear. He walked back toward the house, set up his fold-out chair next to the screened-in porch, and sat down.

"Are you going to sit there all day?" Alice called out the window.

"He'll be out before long," Paddy called back.

"Won't you scare him off?" Alice asked.

"Hrumph," Paddy mumbled.

Alice shook her head and closed the window.

Catching groundhogs is harder than you'd think. Paddy sat out in the yard all morning, getting up only to use the facilities or drag his chair out of the sun, which kept climbing higher in the sky. Once, Paddy shuffled over to the hole beneath the shed and leaned over it to peer inside.

The groundhog never came out. Paddy couldn't believe it. That varmint had shown up every single morning for the past month. Alice finally convinced her husband to come inside for lunch, but when he sat down at the table, all he could do was complain bitterly about the varmint. He took one bite out of his bologna, lettuce, and tomato sandwich, and then looked up and out the window and almost choked.

The groundhog was there, poking its head out from its hole under the shed. The animal slowly emerged and started sniffing its way toward the garden. Paddy stood too quickly and got tangled up with his chair. He also knocked over his water glass, and Alice grabbed a paper towel from the roll next to the kitchen faucet and threw it onto the table as she righted the glass.

"For heaven's sake, you're going to scare him off!" she exclaimed as Paddy headed straight for the door.

Of course, Paddy ignored her. He opened the back door and reached for his chair, scraping it across the grass and stumbling into it. The groundhog, who had reached the garden fence by then, paused and looked up, turning its head toward Paddy. Their eyes locked.

Paddy curled his trembling right hand into a fist, raised it, and shook it at the groundhog. "I've got you now, varmint!" he yelled.

Then, unable to contain himself, he got up and started shuffling toward the creature. The groundhog, startled, dashed away from the garden, but instead of heading back into the safety of its hole, it ran to the opposite side of the yard, seeking escape. Paddy went after it, and when the animal found itself face-to-face with the fence, it was forced to take a right and waddle up the driveway and into the street.

Cars can appear faster than you'd think. A maroon sedan came barreling around the corner at the top of the hill and turned onto the street, music blaring from its open windows. The groundhog froze in the center of the street. Paddy, seeing the car, felt a white-hot rage rise inside him. He stepped out into the street and started yelling at the driver, shaking his fist in the air the way he'd just been shaking it at the groundhog. The driver was a teenage boy who had thick, spiky hair and a girl dancing to the music in the passenger seat. He couldn't have cared less about an animal in the street, but when he saw the old man, he slammed on his brakes. The car skidded to a stop.

"Who the hell do you think you are?" Paddy yelled. "The speed limit is 25 miles an hour on this street!"

The driver managed to both grin and look sheepish. He yelled at Paddy across the passenger seat, saying, "Sorry, old man!" before screeching down the hill, music still blaring, the girl giggling as she looked back at Paddy.

Paddy glared at the car until it turned and disappeared. Then he remembered why he was there in the first place. He looked at center of the street. There was no sign of the groundhog, dead or alive. Paddy scanned the opposite curb, but he didn't see the varmint there, either. So he turned and shuffled back toward the house.

Alice was still sitting at the kitchen the table. "What happened?" she asked.

"He'll be back," Paddy said. He settled back into his chair and reached for what was left of his sandwich.

"What do you mean, 'he'll be back?'"

"He ran across the street."

"Well, that's good, then," Alice said. "Maybe he'll stay there."

"Hrumph," Paddy said.

After the street incident, Paddy went outside every morning to put fresh cantaloupe cubes in the trap. He sat on his chair for three straight days, getting up only for lunch and when the air cooled enough for him to putter in his garden. The groundhog never showed.

"I thought you'd be happy; the whole point was to get rid of him," Alice said to a grumpy Paddy, who had returned to the house in defeat after the third day.

He sat at the kitchen table and waited for his wife to place dinner in front of him. Alice's back had been bothering her, making it harder to cook complete meals. Janie worked most evenings, so she'd signed her parents up for Meals on Wheels, which Paddy now qualified for. Alice split a single meal between the two of them.

"All he did was run across the street," Paddy said. "Where's he going to go? Ray's yard?

He'll come back."

Alice didn't answer.

"It would be better if I could catch him and take him to the cemetery," Paddy insisted.

"That's further away from the house."

Alice stood and picked up the empty foil tray. She carried it over to the sink, and the sound of rushing water filled the silence as she rinsed it off.

Finally, she spoke. "Again, honey, maybe you sitting out there is what is scaring him off."

"Hrumph," Paddy answered.

The next morning, Paddy said he'd heard it might rain, so he'd better watch for the groundhog from the kitchen. Alice could swear the weatherman had predicted a sunny day, but she said nothing. Paddy sat at the table and stared out the window. Alice placed a mug of coffee in front of him.

The truth was, Paddy hated being cooped up inside. He never talked about his time as a POW, not even to Alice. He just told people he liked being outside. He said that walls separated him from the great, wide world, even though that world was getting less great and less wide every year.

Groundhogs are more determined than you'd think. Two mornings later, after Paddy baited the trap and returned to the house for breakfast, the fat, brown body waddled down the driveway, crossed the yard, and headed toward the shed.

"He's back!" Paddy declared, and he rose out of his chair. Alice's back was to the window, so she looked over her shoulder and saw the groundhog dive into its hole.

Paddy headed for the door, but this time Alice raised her voice and said sternly, "Patrick Michael Sullivan, I'll tie you to that chair if I have to!" That stopped Paddy in his tracks.

With a "hrumph," he turned and sat back down.

Alice turned her chair so she could see out the window and watch the proceedings. A few minutes later, the groundhog poked its head out from under the shed. It sniffed the air, looked toward the house, and then slowly and carefully made its way toward the garden. At one point, it stopped to nibble some grass, staring at the house the whole time.

"I'm here, varmint," Paddy muttered. "You just can't see me."

It took a good ten minutes for the groundhog to make it to the garden fence. It sniffed the fence, glanced toward the house again, and then dove into the tunnel, emerging on the other side.

Without much ado, it began munching on the peas. Alice gave Paddy a warning look every time she heard a scraping sound beneath his chair.

Eventually, the groundhog grew tired of the peas and showed some interest in the scent wafting from the trap. It sniffed the air, made its way toward the contraption, and smelled every inch of metal while Paddy's rear inched closer to the edge of his chair. Finally, the groundhog poked its head inside the trap. It paused before placing one paw and then another further inside as it advanced toward the cantaloupe.

Paddy stood up. His eyes never left the window. Alice watched, too, as the groundhog sniffed at the cantaloupe and finally placed a paw gingerly on the trigger.

Groundhogs are bigger than you'd think. When the door fell, half of the groundhog's rump was still sticking out of the trap. The groundhog flailed around in a panic, dragging the trap along with it. After rolling all over the cucumbers and squash, the animal managed to break free.

"Damn it!" Paddy said, slapping both of his hands hard on the windowsill.

"Well," Alice said, "That was a waste of good cantaloupe."

The groundhog waddled rapidly to the garden fence. It dove into the tunnel and emerged on the other side before dashing toward its home under the shed.

That's when Paddy and Alice saw the coyote.

"What the devil—" Paddy shouted from inside the kitchen. Alice froze.

The coyote had squeezed through the spot where the maple tree grew in the path of the back fence. It must have heard the groundhog's struggle or seen movement through the fence; it raced straight toward the smaller creature and grabbed it by the neck.

Old men with Parkinson's can move faster than you'd think. It was like time disappeared, and Paddy remembered the body he'd had as a young soldier—strong, lithe, and fast. He was outside in a flash, grabbing a rock from the driveway and throwing it hard at the coyote's head. The rock hit its mark. Stunned, the animal yelped in surprise, dropped the groundhog from its mouth, and then sprinted straight past Paddy down the driveway and up the hill.

Paddy watched the coyote disappear, and then turned to see the groundhog lying on its side in the grass. It wasn't moving. Paddy took a few steps toward the inert creature and saw what appeared to be a small smear of blood on the animal's neck. Paddy stopped. He watched the animal's side for any sign of breath. There was none.

Suddenly, the groundhog's side rose, and then fell. It rose and fell again. Slowly, the groundhog came back to life. It rolled over onto its feet, took a few unsteady steps, and then, picking up speed, sprinted to its hole under the shed and disappeared.

Paddy didn't move for a long time. He just stood in the middle of the yard and stared at the groundhog's hole. Alice watched through the window.

Finally, Paddy turned and walked back into the house, his body feeling sore and old again.

When Alice woke the next morning, Paddy was gone. Alice got up, pulled on the robe Janie had given her for Christmas and stepped into her tattered old house slippers.

She walked down the hall, glancing at the open door of the bathroom on her way.

"Paddy?" she called, but no one answered.

Nothing in the kitchen looked disturbed; Paddy hadn't made himself coffee or toast. Alice walked over to the window and looked out. There was Paddy, sitting in his chair in the middle of the yard, staring at his vegetable garden.

Alice tied the belt of her robe and went outside. The air was cool, and the grass beneath her slippers was damp with morning dew. A flock of sparrows chirped noisily in the bushes at the back of the yard, and a cardinal flitted from one branch to another in the maple tree. A honking noise came from somewhere above, and Alice looked up to see seven Canada geese flying high over the phone wires in a "V" shape.

Paddy was wearing sweatpants, his red flannel robe, and an old pair of yellow work boots. Alice approached his chair, but he held up his hand as if warning her to keep still. She followed his gaze toward the garden, where the gate in the new fence stood open. The groundhog was inside.

Paddy and Alice didn't speak. They just breathed the morning air, listened to the birds, and watched the groundhog eat the last of the peas.

# CAPTURE
# THE MOON

Jim steered his car into the vacant parking lot, sorry to disturb the fresh blanket of snow.

To him, the night snow was like a blank canvas, now marred by the tires of his Subaru Outback. He found the sign marking the trailhead and parked directly in front of it. His headlights illuminated the large, painted letters: "Mount Carson. Rock Creek Trail."

Carson was more of a foothill, really, especially compared to Prince Peak. Prince loomed large on the other side of the valley, a 13-er, known for its spiked rocky summit. That's why Jim was here. He loved the craggy aesthetics of Prince, especially in silhouette against the moonlit night sky. But he also had a soft spot for quiet hills like Carson, and he liked Rock Creek Trail, named for the narrow waterway that drained the mountain's snowmelt every spring. Jim had hiked the trail many times, and he would have no problem navigating it in the middle of the night, no matter what Elise had said.

Anyway, this was what she wanted, right? "You're not the same man I married," she'd said.

Well, here I am, Jim thought, doing something crazy out-doors. Living large, doing my thing, just me and my camera and the mountains.

The snowstorm ended earlier that night, but a few flakes still drifted toward the ground. Jim cut the car's ignition, inhaled a deep breath, and sat still for a moment, absorbing the silence as he waited for the headlights to go dark. It was warm inside the car, but an icy blast would greet him as soon as he opened the door. Jim was okay with that. Winter weather didn't bother him, and neither did the darkness. He was inspired by the challenge of meeting nature where it was. He liked the rewards earned by pushing through discomfort: fresh trails—blazed with skis or snowshoes—moments of near silence in the middle of the woods, and unexpected encounters with curious wild-life. Being bold was how he captured the rare scenes few others witnessed. *At least*, Jim thought, *that's how I used to capture them.*

Tonight, to protect himself from the frigid elements, Jim wore a ten-year-old fleece jacket, Polartec long johns underneath his blue jeans, lightweight high-top hiking boots, and the black cap Elise knitted for him. He tugged off his gloves, which he wouldn't need when his body warmed during the uphill trek, and shoved them into his left pocket. Then he secured his headlamp to his forehead, just in case. He didn't switch it on; he likely wouldn't need it on a moonlit night. He opened the door and climbed out of the car, slammed the door shut, secured all the locks with a click of his fob, and zipped his keys securely into his right pocket. He barely felt the weight of the camera around his neck, the telephoto lens stored in his backpack, or the tripod secured to the pack with the straps that he usually used to carry his skis.

As Jim started up the trail, the echo of Elise's protests intruded on his solitude. "Are you crazy?" she'd asked when he had stood up, frustrated, and marched out of the living room, pulling his sweater back over his head along the way.

Elise had followed him into the bedroom and watched in disbelief as he dressed to go out and packed up his gear. "It's freezing out there. It's almost midnight!" she'd said.

Jim hadn't responded; that was the only way he could handle his wife's more emotional moments. Shut her out. Disengage. Close his eyes and hope the conflict would just go away.

Tonight it hadn't worked. He'd left the house with both of them still angry.

Thinking of Elise now, Jim wondered if he was crazy, but not for the reasons she claimed. He sighed and shook his head, tried to force himself to focus on the moment. His breath felt heavy as he trudged up the trail, even labored when he hit the steeper portions. "Steeper" was an embellishment, of course; Rock Creek was a pretty easy trail. Still, Jim couldn't take anything for granted, not outside on a cold winter night hiking up even a small mountain. There was a time, not long ago, when he could have jogged the entire mile to the summit of Carson without breaking much of a sweat. Now he was breathing hard just a few minutes into the hike.

He trudged on. The spot where he planned to stop—a clearing just off the trail that had a wide, open view of the sky and Prince Peak—was only a half-mile up. The darkness hardly slowed him. The full moon transformed the lodgepole pines that surrounded him into eerie silver ghosts. Smatterings of stars were visible through gaps in the canopy. As Jim had expected, the moon illuminated the trail.

The fresh taste of mountain air and the scent of damp dirt, vaguely detectable even on a frozen night, helped calm Jim's mind. Still, he felt stung by the angry words Elise hurled at him before he left.

"You're not the same person you were when we met," she'd said. "You're not even the man I married five years ago."

*Of course I'm not who I was when we met*, Jim thought. Thirteen years ago he'd been a college student about to venture forth. It was easy, back then, to just ski and hike, and take photographs through life. His biggest concern was passing his final exams.

We were young," Jim had responded, noticing the sick feeling that rose in his gut when he said it.

"Jim, we're thirty-five years old."

Jim argued with her again in his mind. *You don't mind the nice cottage we live in do you? You work part-time and do your pottery all afternoon; I'm responsible for paying the rent.*

Jim had been lucky, in fact, that he'd had a knack for computers. His artistic bent helped him move seamlessly into the field of interface design. He hadn't taken many photographs in recent years, but he had created some kick-ass UI designs. He could spend hours finessing the pixels on an icon. Should he put a 1.5px bevel on the edge to catch the light? Keep it flat? To Jim, these things had become as important as determining the best angle to capture the moon.

Elise had brought up his photography during the fight. "I can't remember the last time you used your camera," she'd said.

She purchased the camera for Jim years ago with money she earned selling glazed mugs and bowls to a pottery store.

Their orange cat, Malcolm, jumped off the couch in the middle of the argument and sauntered down the hall toward the bedroom. The cat hated raised voices.

When Jim reminded Elise of his similar discomfort, she'd said, "Oh please, Jim. Life is messy. If you're too comfortable, you're missing something. You're the one who used to tell *me* that."

When Elise's words hit too close to the truth, Jim's instinct was always to strike back. "You wouldn't be too comfortable missing your health insurance," he'd retorted.

In an instant, her anger had turned to pain. He could tell by the sudden silence, by the tears that welled up in her eyes.

"So you're saying it's my fault you took the job." she'd said, the fire gone.

"I didn't say that."

It was too late. A tear slipped down Elise's cheek.

A thin layer of sweat had already formed underneath Jim's jacket and sweater. When he stopped walking, he would definitely feel the chill. He gulped the frigid air into his lungs, hoping to ease the tightness that gripped his chest. He curled and released his fists to keep the blood pumping and continued his methodical ascent. He didn't want to think about the argument anymore. He got the point. For the past year he'd been spending more time at work, and when you added in the forty-five-minute commute, he'd hardly been home. Maybe he *had* changed, but did that have to be a bad thing?

For years, when he'd worked as a consultant from home, he and Elise had counted every dollar. She didn't seem to mind, but Jim wanted more. For one thing, he wanted to buy a house. When the subject of having a child came up, Jim experienced a new kind of pressure. The child hadn't come, at least not yet, but their financial struggles continued until he took this job. It was the first real job he'd ever had, and he was surprised at the way it felt to be a productive member of society. He enjoyed watching their bank balance grow. He liked taking paid vacations. He even got a kick out of manipulating the investments he was making in his 401(k).

*Our 401(k),* Jim reminded himself. Elise was benefiting from this job as much as he was, wasn't she? She wanted him to take pictures? Well, before he took this job he had sold eight framed photographs. The money he'd earned as a photographer wouldn't pay one month's rent.

Despite his warm torso, Jim's nose and forehead were beginning to sting with cold. I should have worn a balaclava, he thought. The sky above him was thick, like velvet, yet paled by the glow of the moon. Jim wondered if it would be possible to photograph that color; it was difficult to create a true portrait of darkness. It was easier to depict something rich with light than to capture the essence of emptiness. He would have to hint at it or come at it sideways somehow.

Involuntarily, Jim reached up and touched his camera.

It hit him like a rock, then, a tension that caused his gut to clench painfully, making it difficult to continue taking breaths. Despite the feeling, Jim forged on. He recognized the sensation as anxiety; a doctor had labeled it after a scary incident last year when Jim believed he was having a heart attack.

*"Hoooo, hooooo."*

The sound echoed through the trees. It stopped him. He listened through the wheeze of his own labored breaths. Jim had always loved the haunting call of an owl. He hoped he wouldn't hear an ensuing scream; Jim accepted nature for what it was, but he was a peaceful guy at heart. Maybe that was why he'd always liked photography; he was fascinated by moments, not what happened before or after. He'd taken dozens of photographs of his friend Leo, an accomplished skier, reaching back to grab the tails of his skis mid-jump; no one knew, when they looked at those photos, if Leo had crashed once he landed. All that mattered was the joy of that moment in the air, the bliss between the trip up and the plunge down.

*"Hoooo, hoooo."*

No screams. Jim's breathing began to relax. He walked on.

He knew his destination the moment he arrived; it was obvious, even at night. A large rock near the side of the trail marked the spot where a clearing opened to the right. At the point where the trees parted, the side of the mountain sloped downward just enough to offer a clear view of the horizon on the opposite side of the valley. Jim stood for a moment and absorbed the impossibly beautiful scene. The edges of bare tree branches trailed toward the clearing, casting shadows on the new-fallen snow. The sky was so vast, the stars so infinite. The moon, positioned just to the right of Prince's summit, displayed itself with the pride of a peacock flaunting its tail.

Jim stepped into the clearing. The snow was a few inches deeper off the trail, but he hardly noticed; his fingers practically itched to snap the image of the full moon. Perfect, he thought. Just perfect.

Stopping, even for a few moments, had chilled Jim's sweat, and his fingers began to burn with cold. Before he could pull on his gloves, he had to set up the tripod, unpack his telephoto lens, and set everything up. It was a relief to swing his pack over his right shoulder and stand it up in the snow. He loosened the outer straps, tugged the tripod free and lengthened each leg until it clicked. Glancing at the moon and quickly around the clearing, he chose a good spot to set up. He had just planted the tripod firmly in the snow and unscrewed his camera's lens cap when he heard it.

Snap.

Jim froze. A twig had cracked near the ground behind him, and in the stillness of the night the sound ricocheted like a gunshot. Jim turned toward the noise. He saw nothing but the trees at the edge of the clearing. He waited a moment. Silence. He must have imagined it.

*Snap.*

This time, the sound was unmistakable. Something was moving in the trees.

A bear, thought Jim. It must be a bear. But in the middle of winter? Kind of strange. Didn't bears hibernate? Jim didn't have any food in his backpack. He hadn't even brought a protein bar. Anyway, he thought, if it's a bear, I know how to deal with it. He pulled back his shoulders and tried to look big—an easy task, since he was almost six feet tall. He would yell and stomp his feet, anything to make noise.

Then he saw it.

It wasn't a bear.

The triangular head, rounded ears, and almond-shaped eyes were unmistakable. It was a mountain lion.

The lion stopped mid-step, its head, shoulders, and one advancing front leg visible in the moonlight at the boundary of the clearing. Shadows enveloped the rest of its body. Jim stared. The great cat stared back. Its head appeared to shimmer beneath the moon, the tawny color washed out to silver. Fifteen feet separated the animal from Jim.

Of course Jim knew about mountain lions, but he'd never seen one. Their numbers had dwindled as more and more towns encroached on their habitat. Jim wasn't as familiar with the protocol for a lion encounter as he was with the procedure for scaring off a bear.

The lion nonchalantly swung another leg forward and emerged from the darkness into the light of the clearing. Another two steps, and the full length of its body became visible.

Jim remained still and tried to remember anything he had heard about how to deal with mountain lions. The part of him that felt comfortable in the wilderness remained calm, but a deeper instinct took hold of his body. A shiver of fear flashed through him. A surge of adrenaline urged him to run, but his mind kept him planted where he was. No human being could outrun a mountain lion.

The lion stared at Jim for a few more moments and then lowered its back haunches and sat down. *Okay, that could be a good thing*, Jim thought. Then a movement near the ground caught his attention. The lion flicked its tail. Not such a good thing.

Jim's chest felt so tight that it occurred to him, once again, that he might be having a heart attack. He forced himself to draw air in through his nose as quietly as possible. The white condensation of his exhaled breath clearly caught the lion's attention. Its tail twitched again.

Jim's mind began to race, and he thought, crazily, of his cell phone. He'd switched it off, as he usually did when he spent time outdoors. Anyway, a phone call might not work too well.

'Excuse me, big guy, big girl, whatever, I need to make a call—Elise? Hi, listen, I'm halfway up Mount Carson, and a mountain lion decided to stop by. Could you help?'

Stay calm, Jim told himself, stay calm. You've been in plenty of scrapes before. What the heck should he do? He couldn't just stand here, or maybe he could. Just wait the animal out. It hadn't attacked. As the word "attacked" crossed his mind, it occurred to Jim for the first time that this could be it—*really* it. These could be the last moments of his life. And that's when it hit him.

This was the opportunity of a lifetime.

The notion was so bizarre, so ridiculous and out of place, that Jim was never able to explain where it came from.

He kept his eyes on the animal as he inched his right hand toward the camera that still hung around his neck. The great cat watched him, but didn't move. A switch flipped in Jim's mind; he was now in photographer mode. The night was dark, yes, but the moonlight cast enough light to capture an image with the automatic setting on his Canon 60D. The telephoto lens was still in the backpack, but he didn't need it for this kind of shot. The 50mm lens on the camera would do the trick. Jim hadn't turned the image stabilization off, because he hadn't mounted the camera on his tripod yet. Should he use a shutter cable release to reduce camera jitter? He might not have a chance to fiddle with that. The night was clear of course, so that was good. He'd love to adjust the shutter speed and the ISO, but he was pretty sure he wouldn't have time. The automatic setting would have to do.

*The cold air must have frozen my brain*, Jim thought. But he had recognized the old feeling the instant it hit him; he was suddenly, shockingly alive. The intensity of the sensation brought home how long it had been since he'd felt this way. His breath began to flow, and he drew in the cold air as if he could actually taste oxygen. The details of the scene—the unearthly splendor of the lion's face, the implied strength of the animal's sinewy shoulders, the deep depressions of Jim's footprints in the snow, the tangled, frosted tree branches casting their spindly shadows toward the center of the clearing—all were suddenly heightened.

The camera touched Jim's face. His right eye and the viewfinder became one. He moved the power switch to "on" with his thumb. The lion hadn't moved, so he had a little time. He chose the "creative" auto setting through the viewfinder, and swiveled the control wheel to select "night scene."

The lion appeared to be watching intently. Jim pressed the shutter halfway down, bringing the great cat into razor-sharp focus. He couldn't resist moving the camera slightly to the right to center the image. The movement seemed to waken something in the lion's eyes, and its tail twitched again. Jim, however, was beyond fear now. Everything vanished but his eye, the cold, slanted cast of the luminescent moonlight, and the lion—the gentle curves of its ears, the dramatic shape of its magnificent eyes, its sharp, jutting cheekbones, the slope of its elongated nose.

The lion was perfection. The lion was life. Jim adjusted the camera once more, and then clicked.

At the sound, the cat's ears swiveled forward. It was on its feet in less than a second, crouched and ready to spring. The camera fell out of Jim's hands. The lion leaped.

Jim arms flew up against his face as he started screaming. The knowledge came to him in a rush, what you're supposed to do if you cross paths with a mountain lion in the woods. Raise your arms, look big, make noise, do whatever it takes to convince the animal that you're not prey. It was too late.

The lion hurtled toward him, growling, and when its front paws hit Jim square in the chest they knocked the precious oxygen out of his lungs. Terror gripped Jim as he fell backwards into the snow. The lion's claws tore into his jacket and its teeth gripped his left arm. A burst of pain shot through Jim as he pounded the lion's shoulders and head with his fists. The tripod was within reach. Jim grabbed one of its legs and swung the whole thing toward the lion. Adrenaline surged through him as the tripod hit its mark. Surprised, the animal growled and released Jim's arm. Jim forgot everything then; he fought with every ounce of strength he had, hitting, screaming, and kicking. He swung the tripod again and this time it hit the lion square in the jaw. The animal withdrew with a howl of pain and retreated, backing up and then turning to sprint toward the trees. Jim lay gasping in the snow. When he looked up, the lion was gone.

Jim didn't care about protocol anymore. He let go of the tripod, scrambled to his feet, and bolted unsteadily through the underbrush toward the trail. Sharp thorns scraped his legs and arms; he slammed head first into a tree. He surged forward again, but tripped over a tree root and stumbled to the ground, smacking his chest against the camera, which still hung on the strap around his neck. He struggled up and kept going, too terrified to look back. As soon as he found the trail he started running. Whether by memory or desperation or the illumination of the moon, Jim found his way down to the base of the mountain.

The snow was falling harder again. Jim's keys were still zipped into his jacket pocket. With trembling hands now stinging with cold and pain, he withdrew the keys and unlocked the car.

He fell into the driver's seat, slammed the door shut, and switched on the ignition. Only then, when he was safely enclosed in his car, did he stop to breathe or think or try to absorb what had happened. He slammed his left foot down onto the clutch, shifted the car into reverse, pressed the gas pedal, and backed up the car. Then he shot out of the parking lot, his tires spinning in the snow, and gunned it down the road toward home.

Jim sat quietly, dazed and aching, as the doctor pulled off her latex gloves. She told the young nurse, who had been standing nearby, to clean and dress Jim's wounds.

She regarded Jim thoughtfully and said, "None of the wounds are deep enough to require stitches, but I'd like you to take an antibiotic to avoid infection."

She scribbled something onto a prescription pad and handed it to Jim. He stared at it blindly. Elise took the paper from him and slid it into her pocket. Their next stop, Elise insisted once they were back in the car, was the police station.

"The police should hear what happened," she said. "If there's a mountain lion roaming around on Carson, people need to know."

Their argument had been forgotten when she found him asleep on the couch that morning, his face covered in scratches and his boots still on. Dried blood stained the couch beneath his left arm. His jacket and camera lay discarded on the floor.

"I don't want to go to the police," Jim whispered now.

His throat was sore. His voice was still hoarse from yelling the night before. Despite the attack, he couldn't bear the thought of the police hunting the lion. The mountains were the lion's home, not his—he was the one who had been stupid enough to go to Carson alone in the middle of the night.

Elise glanced at him. "Neither of us wants anything to happen to the lion," she said softly, "but it attacked you, Jim. That makes it dangerous, and families use that trail all the time. What if that lion attacks a child? Do you want that on your conscience? At least they need to put up a sign."

Jim couldn't argue with that.

The police station, a redbrick building on the edge of town, was quiet when Jim entered with Elise. A receptionist behind a glass-paneled half wall pointed them toward a door. The door opened to a sunlit room lined with utilitarian desks. A uniformed police officer stood when they entered and introduced himself as Officer Davis. He waved them into the chairs facing the desk nearest the door. He appeared to be about their age.

The policeman listened to Jim's story and jotted down notes.

"Would you mind showing me the bite marks on your arm?" he asked, surveying the scratches and bruises on Jim's face.

Elise sat quietly as Jim shrugged off his coat, rolled up his sleeve, and pulled up the gauze that covered his deepest wounds.

After a moment, Officer Davis asked, "Are you sure it was a lion? It must have been dark up there."

Jim nodded, and described the animal in detail. "The moon was full last night. There was plenty of light," he explained.

Officer Davis listened thoughtfully. Elise reached over and carefully taped the gauze back into place before sliding Jim's sleeve back to his wrist.

"Can you give me a second?" the policeman asked. Jim nodded.

Officer Davis stood up and walked to the back of the room, where he spoke quietly to the only other policeman on duty. The second officer, a paunchy, weatherworn man, listened intently before squinting across the room at Jim. Then he picked up his telephone and made a call. A minute later, both officers approached Jim and Elise.

"I'm Officer Jackson," the older policeman said. "Listen," he asked Jim, "are you sure what you tangled with was a lion?"

"Yeah," Jim said.

Both officers studied him. "Son," Officer Jackson said, "No one has seen a mountain lion in Adams County for thirty years."

"Do you think it wandered here from somewhere else?" Jim asked.

"There's almost no chance of that," the policeman responded. "A few years ago the folks over at SDEP—"

"The State Department of Environmental Protection," Officer Davis inserted.

"Right," Officer Jackson said. "They wanted to reintroduce the species 25 miles north of here, up in the national park. There was a big hubbub about it, you know, the ranchers and local families worried about lions roaming around the mountains again. The area was pretty remote, but the idea got voted down. That ranger, what's his name?"

"Dave Jefferson," Officer Davis offered.

"Right," the older policeman said. "Jefferson. He's obsessed with the whole idea. The ecosystem and all that. He tried it twenty years ago, when he was new in town, right near Mount Carson in fact. The area was more rural then. But the cat they released got killed. Some idiot shot the thing dead. Claimed he thought it was a deer, but no one believed him."

Jim and Elise sat in a confused silence.

"But I know it was a lion," Jim said.

Then he remembered. "I took a picture. With my camera."

"You took a picture?" the officers asked in unison.

"Before the thing attacked you?" Officer Jackson added, incredulous.

"I know it was stupid," Jim said, "but I did."

"Well, I'd like to see that," Officer Jackson replied, shaking his head. "Go home and rest, son. If you've really got a picture, bring it by later."

Elise and Jim rode home in silence. Just before Elise took the final turn toward their house, Jim stopped her by saying, "Wait. Head out to the park."

"Why?" Elise asked.

"My tripod is up there. My backpack. We need to get them."

"Are you kidding, Jim?"

"Come on," Jim said. "It's broad daylight, and it's only half a mile. I just want to get my stuff."

Elise drove to the park.

Jim's backpack sat where he'd left it, and his tripod still lay on its side in the snow. Elise found Jim's gloves; they had fallen from his pocket during the struggle with the lion. It was obvious where Jim had crashed through the underbrush; a pathway of trampled branches led from the clearing to the trail. A few small bloodstains were visible in the snow. A scrap of material from the sleeve of Jim's jacket hung on one of the branches.

Jim was grateful when Elise said nothing about the obvious. There were no paw prints anywhere in the snow.

After they returned home, Jim picked his camera up off the floor. Somehow the power had been turned off last night; he turned it back on and viewed the stored photo on the LCD screen. There it was: the clearing illuminated by the moonlight. There was nothing between the camera and the trees but fresh snow.

Elise set a mug of coffee on the table next to Jim. She glanced at the camera in his hands. "I never asked you what you were doing up there in the first place," she said. "You ran out of here in the middle of our argument."

Jim looked at her and said, "I wanted to capture the moon."

Elise smiled at him gently and replied, "I think you did."

# WHO LET THE CATS OUT?

There are two things I've never told anyone. But before I can tell those two things to you, I have to tell you the rest of the story. Then maybe there's a chance you'll believe me. So let me back up a few months to the day right after the fire.

I was standing alone in the old Victorian house that once belonged to Jane S. Dooley. It was hard to remember what the living room looked like before the fire that engulfed it the night before. The morning sun streamed in through the bay window that looked out over the front yard and the neatly trimmed bushes in front of the sidewalk. But everything inside—the mantel above the fireplace, the wallpaper with its pattern of delicate flowers, the wood floors, the furniture, the shattered flower vase—was charred and stained, blackened and peeling, covered with ashes.

I had no idea if I would be able to recover the key, and for reasons I didn't understand at the time, the thought inspired a feeling of panic. The floor-to-ceiling bookcase had fallen over and cracked into several pieces, and dozens of sodden books, wet from the hoses of the firefighters, were scattered

across the floor. Some had lost their covers and were par-
tially burned; others had singed pages that curled toward
the bindings.

I spotted one edge of the old hardcover beneath what
remained of the wooden coffee table. The cover of the
book had been a prominent red, making it easy to spot
in the morning sunlight. I kneeled on the floor, pulled the
book from underneath the table, and brushed a light layer
of ashes off the cover. The book was the only thing in the
room that had been mine. *Crime and Punishment* by Fyo-
dor Dostoyevsky. I opened it and saw the key, still there,
taped inside the front cover. I sighed with relief. I loosened
the tape, removed the key, and slipped it into my pocket.

"Adalyn?"

Slamming the book shut, I stood up so quickly that
I slipped on the debris that covered the damp floor. My
assistant, Billy, stepped through the doorway and caught
my arm before I fell. I thanked him with embarrassment and
clutched the book to my chest with one hand, while I used
the other to wipe the soot off the knees of my cargo pants.

"It's a mess, isn't it?" I said, looking up at Billy, who was
eight inches taller than me.

Billy smiled sadly. The apartment had been his home
for nearly a year, since he'd accepted the job of Assistant
Director of the Jane S. Dooley Sheltering Home for Cats. A
rent-free apartment came with the job. The shelter's office
was at the other end of a hallway outside his living room
door, and three upstairs rooms served as living space for
a number of cats while they waited for permanent homes
with local families. Another twenty cats, the ones who got
along well in a larger group, were housed cage-free inside a
spacious cement Cat House that had been built behind the
old Victorian at the end of the driveway.

Loose jeans and a black T-shirt hung on Billy's thin frame, and his short hair, dyed jet black, was messy or spiked with some kind of hair product, I could never tell which. One of his eyebrows was pierced, and he had somehow found the time—even on a morning like this—to apply the touch of dark eyeliner that always made his blue eyes stand out. When people first met Billy, especially people who lived in a small Vermont town like Pineville, they usually raised their eyebrows and assumed all the wrong things. They never suspected that he not only had a heart of gold, but also was a musical genius. He could play Mozart as well as he belted out the grunge rock tunes he performed with his band, "Black Buzzard," every Friday and Saturday night. This job was just a way for Billy to make money and have a free place to live while he finished his master's thesis in music education.

Now, that free place to live, this apartment inside the house that Jane S. Dooley had left to the town as a cat shelter a hundred and fifty years before, had been torched.

Billy glanced around the room. I knew that he'd weathered times worse than this; his mother had died when Billy was young, leaving his father to raise Billy and run their horse ranch on his own. It was one of the things Billy and I had in common even though, at thirty-four, I was ten years older than him. We were both raised by single fathers. I had returned to town two years ago to be with my dad before he died, thinking I'd only stay long enough after he was gone to close up the house and sell it. My life had been at a crossroads at the time; I'd been living in Colorado and the software company I worked for as an office manager had been sold to a larger company. When the director of the Dooley Cat Shelter got married and moved out of town, I decided to stay and apply for the job.

"You're taking this pretty well," I told Billy, trying to convince myself that I also spoke for me.

At exactly the same time, our eyes strayed toward the piano that Billy had moved into the apartment with the rest of his things. It had been a shiny brown upright with gleaming white and black keys, but now it was covered with soot and had visible water damage, and a large dark spot was burned into the side that stood closest to the window. The burning rag soaked in gasoline had landed right next to the piano when it crashed through the window, which the firemen had temporarily boarded up.

"It's insured," Billy said with a shrug. "I'm safe, the cats are safe, Michelle is safe. That's all that matters." Michelle, a local nursing student whose smile lit up the shelter whenever she came by, was Billy's girlfriend.

It's not as if we didn't know that a certain element in town had been grumbling about the shelter. That element consisted mostly of Doris Nelson, the woman who moved into the house next door five years before, and the town's Mayor, Henry Carbunkle. Mayor Henry, as I called him because he hated what he called my impertinence, had, over the previous year, made it his personal mission to shut the shelter down. I had no idea why at first; Henry—who is in his mid-forties—has lived in Pineville all his life, and had been mayor for the last ten years. He'd never had a problem with the shelter before. We suspected that it had something to do with Doris, who complained about everything from Billy's piano playing—which she claimed she could hear from inside her house—to what time we rolled the garbage bins out to the curb every Sunday, and whether or not our driveway was plowed in the winter. She installed a tall wooden fence between her driveway and the shelter's, and that was fine with us. The less we saw of Doris Nelson, the better.

Unfortunately for Doris and Mayor Henry, most of Pineville's small population love and support the shelter. Many local families have found beloved pets at Dooley, or turn to us for help when an elderly relative passes away and leaves a cat in need, or when someone finds a hungry stray by the side of the road.

"Should you be in here, Addy?" Billy and I both turned at the sound of the all-too-familiar voice.

Mayor Henry was standing at the door that led into the living room, and I wondered why he had felt he had the right to walk right into my office, never mind down the hall to the apartment.

"Tom said we could come in," I said, referring to the local fire chief. I stood up a little straighter and made sure my voice was firm. "Why are you *here*?" I asked.

He ignored my question. "I imagine this place is a goner," he said, raising his eyebrows as he looked around the room.

He was six foot four and, in my opinion, an overgrown bully who always wore a cowboy hat and boots as if he thought he lived in Texas and was a sheriff instead of a mayor.

"Actually," I said, "only this room was damaged by the fire. There's just water damage in the kitchen and bedroom. The office is fine, and the upstairs is fine." He shrugged. Feeling angrier, I added, "And I'm sure you'll be happy to hear that Billy saved all of the cats who live upstairs. You do realize that Billy was in here last night, when someone threw a flaming rag soaked in gasoline through the window. He could have been killed."

I noticed a flash of surprise in the Mayor's eyes. "I thought you played with your band on Saturday nights," he said.

"Oh you did?" I asked, suddenly suspicious. I took a step toward him and Billy put a cautioning hand on my arm.

"Now why were you keeping track of Billy's nights out, Mayor Henry?"

I might stand five foot two and weigh all of a hundred and fifteen pounds, but everyone in Pineville knows I'm no pushover. Once, in the tenth grade, I'd punched a kid in the face when he'd made a snide remark about a quiet boy who didn't have a lot of friends. My father had promised the principal I would be punished for my actions, but when we got in the car so he could drive me home, he held up a hand and gave me a "high five."

"I'm only saying I had no idea Billy was home last night," the Mayor said, involuntarily taking a step backwards. He had recovered from his surprise and was back on the offensive. "Had I known, I would have asked if he was alright."

"Right, just like you asked about the cats," I said. "Whoever did this, even if they thought they were doing it when Billy was out, must have known they were going to kill ten innocent cats."

The Mayor's face looked as if it had turned to stone. "Well, *whoever did this* might not have even known this place is a cat shelter," he replied smoothly.

"And where were you last night, Mayor Henry?" I asked. "Your life's mission for the past year has been to shut down the shelter."

"You have to be kidding me," he said, getting angry again. "I'm the Mayor of this town, and I have better things to do than to try to burn down someone's house or a cat shelter. I spent the entire evening with my wife, in fact, at Buddy's Grill and the cinema center in Layton."

"Will the police be able to find out who did do this?" Billy asked, interrupting our heated exchange. He gestured toward the piano. "There's been a lot of damage, and the truth is, sir, that

I *could* have been killed, and the cats could have been, too."

The mayor shrugged again. "It was probably someone teenager on a dare," he said. "I'm sure Sam will do his best to find out." Sam Reynolds was the local police chief.

Sam and Henry were thick as thieves; I had no doubt that if Henry Carbunkle was behind this fire, his buddy Sam wouldn't do anything about it.

"Well, good luck to you," Mayor Henry said, turning on his boot heel before walking back down the hall and out of the house. I heard the office door slam.

"Look, Addy," Billy said, his voice sounding tired, "I appreciate the invitation to stay at your house while this gets sorted out, but I'm perfectly happy to sleep on the floor of the office."

"No way," I said. "I'm going to sleep in that office tonight and every night until they find out who did this and get the apartment back in shape."

Billy nodded and walked toward the entrance to the bedroom, where I knew he had to retrieve some of his things. But before he left the room, he stopped and turned toward me. "Addy," he said, "there's something I should tell you."

"What?" I asked.

"Last night, before the fire, something woke me up."

"Did you hear people talking, or a car outside the house?"

Billy hesitated. "No." he said, "It was the piano. Someone was playing the piano."

"WHAT?" I exclaimed. "Who?"

"I don't know. But I heard the piano; just a few notes. The sound woke me out of a deep sleep, and then I heard it again. I got up and came into the living room to see who was here, thinking maybe it was Michelle. But when I got here, there was no one. The piano was just sitting there. And then a few seconds later I heard a crash and that burning rag came flying through the window." He shook his head as if he still couldn't believe what he had seen.

"The flames moved so fast," he said apologetically. "The curtains caught fire. I tried to pull them down and stomp on them, but it didn't work. The fire just kept spreading. I ran into the kitchen and grabbed the fire extinguisher, but by the time I got back in here half the room was up in flames, so I grabbed my cell and called 911 while I ran upstairs to get the cats. And it was weird; someone had opened the doors to all the rooms as if they wanted to let the cats out. All ten of them were in the hall near the carriers. I think that's why I was able to save them all."

We both stood quietly for a moment, remembering the hours that had followed that call:

the sirens, the chaos, the fear for the animals still locked in the Cat House. I was still holding my copy of *Crime and Punishment*, and I subtly patted my pocket, feeling for the key. It was still there.

"That's strange," I said. "Maybe some jokester snuck into the house before lighting the place on fire. It doesn't really make sense. But if he—or she—comes back, I'll be waiting."

The Jane S. Dooley Cat Shelter was established in 1837 by an elderly Pineville resident who had inherited her father's fortune and had no close relatives on whom to bequeath it. She had been married as a young woman, but her husband died of a terrible fever; she never re-married or had children. According to local legend, Jane used to stroll up and down Main Street on warm summer days, delighting the town's children by handing out candy. She started a women's book club at the tiny town library and gave generously to neighbors in need. But her passion was animals, especially cats. When she died at the ripe old age of ninety-seven, she left all of her fortune, including the large Victorian house she had called home, in a trust for the establishment of a sheltering home for cats.

So the residents of Pineville, mourning their elderly neighbor, founded the cat shelter that Jane envisioned. And no one had ever had a problem with the shelter before Doris Nelson moved next door and began her insidious attempt to close it down. Of course, Doris had been the first person I'd thought of as flames threatened to devour Jane Dooley's house. I had demanded that Dave Miller, a local policeman who was keeping the neighbors back and whom I knew I could trust, knock on Doris' door to find out if she'd had anything to do with the fire. But Doris, it turned out, was visiting relatives in Boston. So she couldn't have started the fire.

The alarm clock I placed on the floor of the office glowed 1:04 a.m. The night was dark, the office was cold, and I was huddled in my sleeping bag, wide awake. October nights can be frigid in Vermont but I didn't like to turn up the heat, so I was wearing a sweat shirt and sweat pants inside the sleeping bag.

I spent the evening working in the office, attempting to sort through the paperwork that would be required to file a claim with the shelter's insurance company. At 10:30 p.m. I tried to turn in because my eyes were starting to hurt and I could no longer concentrate. I did a final check of the Cat House and confirmed that all nineteen residents were sleeping on cat beds in the specially-designed windowsills, nibbling at the kibble that had been left out in bowls, or chasing each other around the floor in the dark. When I left, I made sure the door was locked, and then I paused next to the shed that backed up to the fence just outside the

Cat House door. The moon was almost full, and the back of the shed was in shadow. In fact, it was there, behind the shed, that I had found Jocko on that terrible night.

Jocko. He had been a handsome, scarred, gray and white tom cat when he appeared in the driveway a few days after I started my job at the shelter. He was huge—twenty pounds—and tough judging by his ears, which were all chewed up, and by the scar on his upper lip that turned his expression into a permanent scowl. It was clear that he had been living on the street for a long time. But he must have decided that he'd had enough, because he marched straight up to the office door and strolled inside that day. And he proceeded, over the next two years, to become the shelter mascot and the most beloved feline on the property. He spent his days lounging in the office and the evenings sleeping peacefully on Billy's bed after I convinced the Board of Directors to let me hire Billy and move him into the apartment.

Jocko was protective of any cats that arrived at the office hungry, scared, and in search of a home. He nudged and groomed young kittens if they cried. And whenever I arrived in the morning for work, he jumped up and unlatched the door from the hallway, sauntered into the office and sat down in front of me, hoping to be petted.

Jocko had been wearing a collar with a tag when he arrived, but no one claimed ownership even though neighbors reported spotting him roaming in the neighborhood near the shelter for years. Even stranger, the tag he wore was very odd—it was silver and heart-shaped and appeared to be a locket of some kind. It had the letter "J" stamped on the front which is why I named the cat Jocko. But whenever I tried to remove the collar so I could open up the locket Jocko hissed, bared his teeth, and unsheathed his claws— behavior he never exhibited at any other time. So the collar remained around Jocko's neck until the tragic events of July 4th.

It was 6:30 a.m. and raining on the morning of the holiday when Jocko raced past my legs as I arrived at the office to take care of some work I wanted to get done on the holiday. He ran down the driveway and behind the shed, and before I could get to him I heard something that sounded like a dog yelping. The next thing I knew I was frozen in horror because a coyote had emerged from behind the shed. It ran right past me up the driveway toward the street, and I raced behind the shed, calling Jocko's name. I found him lying on his side in the dirt behind the shed with blood seeping out of his neck.

Next to him was a tiny white kitten, not more than a few weeks old, cowering against the shed, untouched. I realized in an instant what had happened: Jocko had attacked the coyote to save the kitten. I fell to my knees and begged Jocko to hold on so I could get him to the emergency vet. But he took a few last breaths, heaved a sigh, and died right there in my arms.

The death of any cat breaks my heart, but I had never taken a death as badly as I took Jocko's. Billy found me sobbing with the cat in my arms, and we buried him later that day in the yard in front of the Cat House. Before we laid him in his grave inside his favorite bed, I took off the collar that he'd never let me touch. I didn't have the heart to open the locket in my grief, so I bought a small gold box and locked the collar inside it. I never told anyone about the box, which I placed in the bottom drawer of my desk at the office, or about the key, which I taped into the inside cover of one of my favorite books, *Crime and Punishment.* I then stored the books among the books in Billy's apartment.

After the fire I realized how close I had come to never being able to open the box and find out what was inside the locket. So after Billy had gone home I had removed the key from my pocket, pulled the box from the drawer, and opened it.

It was empty.

Sleep continued to elude me. I couldn't stop thinking about the fire, about the fact that Billy could have been killed, about the helpless cats who had been upstairs, about Mayor Henry's visit. I went over and over our conversation in my head, trying to pick out anything that would indicate he was responsible. And finally, when my thoughts had raced in circles for so long that they had to land somewhere, I thought about Jocko's empty box, which was now sitting next to the alarm clock on the floor. Twenty minutes had passed since I'd last looked at the clock.

And that's when I heard it.

*Plink, plink, plink.* At first it was one note, then two, then a slow crescendo as someone ran his or her fingers up the piano keys. I grabbed the flashlight and struggled up and out of my sleeping bag. Trying to control my ragged breath, I crept on my tip-toes through the door that led to the hallway and made my way toward the apartment. The door to the living room was open, even though I was certain I had closed it after Billy left. I clicked off the flashlight and moved toward the door quietly, guided by a sliver of moonlight shining through the open door.

I peeked through the door and looked across the room to the piano, but no one appeared to be there. The piano was silent and the shadowy room, eerily lit by the light of the moon, was empty. I walked into the apartment over to the bay window, listening for footsteps or any other sound and keeping my flashlight off. Nothing. No one. Confused, I stared out the window. And then I saw, out of the corner of my eye, what looked like a person running away from the house. I ran into the front foyer, unbolted the front door, and raced down the walkway to the sidewalk, forgetting that it was freezing outside and my feet were bare. I stared in the direction where I had seen the person running, but saw nothing but darkness past the streetlight on the corner. Whoever it was had disappeared.

Two weeks later on a Thursday night, the meeting of the town council was a mob scene. Every seat in the Town Hall meeting room was taken, and men, women, and children were lined up along the walls and milling around the hallway just outside the double doors. Mayor Henry rapped his wooden gavel against the podium in a vain attempt to quiet the angry crowd. His wife was sitting in the front row with their two children, twelve-year-old Jimmy and ten-year-old Janine. She stared blankly at her husband, and the children hung their heads and stared at the floor.

The mayor had just announced that the Jane Dooley house was condemned. The insurance company had mysteriously turned down our initial claim, saying they suspected that the fire had been a ploy to get money for the shelter by collecting on the policy. I was outraged at this implication, which made no sense. But to make matters worse, the Mayor declared that because there were no other locations in town suitable for a cat shelter, the shelter would have to be shut down. Rumors had been circulating for days that this was his plan, and supporters of the shelter had vowed to show up at the meeting and make their feelings known.

"What about the cats?" someone yelled from the middle of the crowd.

"They'll be sent to shelters in nearby towns," the mayor said, "and if any are left without a place to go, they'll have to be put down."

There was a roar of anger from the crowd. I was shaking with rage, and Billy and Joanne Watkins, two of our most loyal volunteers, were each pulling at one of my arms as I stood at a microphone stand that had been placed in front of the audience, shouting.

"What do you mean, condemned?" I shouted. "One room has smoke and fire damage. The rest of the building is sound. What are you talking about? You'll harm one hair on one cat over my dead body!"

"According to the town inspector—" the mayor began, but his comments were drowned out by more shouts from the crowd.

Billy dragged me back to my seat in the seventh row, where I collapsed into my chair, uncertain if I would be able to stop the angry tears that had sprung to my eyes. I couldn't believe what was happening.

"Who set the fire?" someone yelled from the crowd, and the question was echoed by a chorus of other voices.

"They need to be held responsible!"

"And who let the cats out from their upstairs rooms?" Someone shouted from the back of the room. "Who knew that the fire was going to be set?"

The Mayor banged his gavel on the podium again until the noise had subsided just enough for him to say, "The police have not found a suspect in the fire. It is the assumption of the insurance company that someone involved with the shelter did the deed to make money, which would explain why the cats were let out." Anything he said after that was drowned out by a general roar of angry objections.

Back at the shelter an hour after the meeting, at least twenty volunteers had gathered under the light above the door of the Cat House, wrapped in jackets, gloves, and hats. Everyone was still angry.

"There's no way we're going to let this happen," Joanne said.

"It's crazy, anyway," said Emily Leblanc, the owner of the local breakfast shop, Toffey Coffee, and a long-time volunteer at the shelter. "Why shut the whole place down even if the house is condemned? The Cat House is still fine, and we could always rebuild."

"There's absolutely no reason to condemn that house," said Eric Horner, a local handyman who did repairs at the shelter and who had recently built an outdoor enclosure for the cats. "The structure is fine. Heck, most of the house is perfectly fine. This is a conspiracy if I ever saw one, and when we find out who started it and who set that fire, there's going to be hell to pay."

I had been sitting in the office, drained from my fury, trying to figure out what to say to everyone. When I finally joined the group Joanne turned to me and said, "If the insurance company won't pay, we can fix the house ourselves."

"There's no way we could raise enough money," I said. The last few hours had drained my fighting spirit, and the reality of what we were facing had kicked in. "Our operating budget doesn't include a line item for repairs, and this is a major job. The shelter is barely making ends meet as it is."

"I'll give up my salary," Billy said. He was standing in the crowd with his hands stuffed in his pockets. Michelle put her arms around him and leaned her head against his chest.

"That's sweet of you, Billy," I said, and I was surprised that my voice cracked when I said it. My throat felt tight and I forced myself to take a deep breath. "But I would never let you do that, and it wouldn't be enough anyway. Believe me, I would give up my salary, too."

A young girl standing in the group with her mother started to cry. Her mom, Audrey

Benson, leaned down and gave her a hug. "It's OK, honey," she said. "Let's go to the Cat House and visit Pepper."

The girl sniffed but looked up hopefully. "Can we take Pepper home now, Mom?" she asked.

Audrey looked at me and I smiled weakly. "Yes, sweetie, I think so," Audrey said. "I think it's time for Pepper to come home."

I knew that her family already had three cats. I nodded at Billy and he unlocked the door of the Cat House before following them inside.

After everyone had left, I lay down once again in my sleeping bag in the office and finally let myself just cry. Between my own sobs I heard the occasional swish of a car driving slowly by on the street. As always, I'd closed all the window blinds. There was no moon that night and the room was pitch black except for the red neon numbers on the alarm clock. The first time I looked at them it was midnight. By one o'clock I had exhausted myself, and my tears had dried. By two o'clock I was falling asleep.

*Plink, plink, plink.* Three notes on the piano. My eyes flew open. *Plink, plink.* Two more. I was out of my sleeping bag in seconds, flashlight in hand. I crept down the hall toward the living room and again was surprised to find the apartment door open. I hurried toward it and this time swung it open quickly and stepped into the room, sweeping the beam of my flashlight from one wall to the next. Finally I pointed it toward on the keys of the piano.

Nothing. No one. But then I heard footsteps from somewhere past the front foyer. I sighed with relief, thinking that Billy had decided to sleep in his room one last time. I crossed the room and entered the foyer.

The front door to the house was wide open. Suddenly on guard, I looked through the doorway to Billy's bedroom and saw what looked like a hooded figure moving around in the shadows. Then I heard a click and a small flame burst to life, illuminating a man facing near the bed. It looked like he was holding a rag in one hand.

"Hey! Stop that!" I yelled, turning on my flashlight.

The man dropped the rag and turned, trying to shade his eyes against the light. I stared back in surprise. The man in the hood—a hooded sweatshirt, it turned out—wasn't actually a man at all. He was twelve years old, and his name was Jimmy Carbunkle.

"Jimmy?" I said in surprise.

The boy dropped the lighter now and dashed toward the front door, but I caught him by his hood and he slid and fell backwards.

"What are you doing here?" I asked. "Are you here to... are you the one who...did your father put you up to this? Did you come back to finish the job?"

Jimmy sobbed as he tried to wriggle out of his sweatshirt and break free. A police siren started wailing and was getting closer to the house. By the time Jimmy had gotten the sweatshirt off and broken loose from my grasp a squad car with revolving lights had pulled onto the curb, and Dave Miller was racing up to the front of the house. He stopped short when he saw Jimmy standing at the front door.

"I decided to park at the end of the street after the meeting," Dave said when he saw my confusion at his arrival. "I was worried there would be trouble. I thought I saw some movement a few minutes ago so I drove a little closer, and then when I saw the flashlight go on inside the house I put on the siren and pulled up."

He looked at Jimmy. "So who do we have here? Jimmy Carbunkle?"

The boy continued to sob. Dave stopped me with a gentle hand when I reached down to pick up the lighter he had dropped. "Evidence," he said, and I left it where it was. "As for you, young man, it looks like I'll be giving you a ride down to the station." Jimmy wiped his eyes with one arm and started to hiccup.

"Wait," I said. "Before you go..." I turned toward Jimmy, who refused to look at me. "Jimmy, tell me why you did this. Why would you want to hurt the shelter and the cats we keep here? I know your father doesn't like Dooley very much, but why would you get involved?"

Jimmy sniffed and stared at the floor. Dave and I waited. Finally, the boy said, "Mom and

Dad keep arguing about this place. Dad says he wants to get rid of it because that new lady, Mrs. Davis, promised to help him get re-elected if he did. My mom was really upset. She said she was tired of my dad pan..pan.."

"Pandering," I said softly.

Jimmy hiccuped again. "Yes, pandering to people who he likes and who can help him, or something like that. She said she knew that my dad was in love with Miss Davis and she was sick of it all and going to leave him. She's said she would leave him before, but this time I think she meant it."

"But why would you try to burn down the shelter?" I asked.

"Dad said some bad things about Billy, about how he was a poor role model for kids in the town anyway, and how he was played with some kind of crazy band on the weekends.

He made jokes about his hair and his makeup and stuff. I just wanted it all to go away. I wanted it to stop, for everything to go back to the way it was before Miss Davis and Billy moved here. I figured since Billy was out of the house on the weekends I could just..just..." his voice faded.

"I think you'd better save the rest until we call your father and he meets us at the station," Dave said. "Let's go." He led Jimmy toward his patrol car and I watched in the light from the street lamp. Just before they reached the sidewalk, Jimmy turned back to look at me.

"I didn't know there were cats in the house," he said. "I thought they were all out back. I didn't know. I never meant to hurt them. I'm sorry!" And he started to cry again. Dave put a firm hand on his shoulder and opened the back door of the squad care before ushering Jimmy inside.

The car drove off into the night.

A week had passed since Jimmy Carbunkle made a full confession. His mother had packed her bags and left Mayor Henry, who had been keeping a very low profile. The local paper had printed at least twenty letters to the editor calling for the mayor's resignation—not because his son had been implicated in a crime or even because of the whispers that he had been having an affair—but because an investigation had unearthed a conspiracy to close down the shelter between the mayor and the town's police chief and fire inspector.

Still, our problems weren't over. The insurance company had agreed to review our claim, but the appeal process was going to take months. We had to repair the main building so that Billy could move back in and there could be 24-hour supervision at the shelter, a town requirement.

Our volunteers had put up donation boxes in every store and were brainstorming about organizing some fundraising events. But I couldn't think of any way we could get the kind of money we needed in the short time we had to save the building and the shelter.

I had continued to sleep on the floor of the office so we would be complying with the town's 24-hour requirement. I just didn't feel right making Billy do it. But my back was beginning to hurt, winter was getting closer, and I knew I couldn't sleep there forever. I lay awake in my sleeping bag late almost every night trying to come up with some kind of a solution. But as the days wore on, and no answer presented itself, I began—in my exhaustion—to consider whether it might be best to focus my energy on finding homes for our remaining cats and preparing to close down, at least temporarily.

Late one night, I was running through the names of the cats in my mind as the light of the moon peeked through the blinds. *Dave might take Midget,* I was saying to myself. *Joanne might open her home to one more. I know she loves little Simba.*

And then I heard it again.

*Plink, plink, plink.*

I was sure I was dreaming in my half-asleep state, but this time the notes kept coming. *Plink, plink, plink, plink, plink,* up the piano keyboard and down again. It was 3:00 a.m. I crawled out of my sleeping back, picked up my flashlight, and walked through the office into the hallway and toward the apartment.

The door was open again.

I closed my eyes, shook my head a few times, and then looked again. Yes, it was open.

And this time I could still hear the notes. *Plink, plink, plink,* faster and faster.

"Billy?" I called out. Silence.

"Who's playing this joke on me?" I said in a loud voice as I pushed the door open and walked hesitantly into the room.

The music stopped, It took a moment for the beam from my flashlight to find the piano. But just as it did, I thought I saw something move. Was it a shadow from the branch of a tree outside? Or was it the flick of a tail? I entered the room and walked over to the piano, but the window was closed and no one was there. Then I stopped dead in my tracks. There was something on the piano keys.

Jocko's collar. I stood frozen, barely able to breathe. Finally I moved forward and picked up the collar and pointed the flashlight at the "J" on the locket. It was time. I opened the locket and something small and shiny glinted in the beam of light.

It wasn't until the diamond was appraised two days later that I realized that the Jane S. Dooley Sheltering Home for Cats had been saved.

Here are the two things I've never told anyone. The first one is this: before I replaced *Crime and Punishment* in the new bookshelf Eric built when the apartment was fully renovated something fell from the middle pages onto the floor. It was an old photograph of Jane Dooley. When I looked closely at the photo I noticed she was wearing something around her neck. It was a locket adorned with the letter "J."

The second thing is this: when I left the apartment on the night I found the diamond, I paused at the door and looked back into the room. I swept the beam of my flashlight from one wall to the other, let it rest on the piano, and then on the floor. And there, for the first time, I noticed something in the soot that I had never noticed before. There were paw prints leading from the piano to the door.

The next morning, the paw prints were gone.

9 798990 504936